Next Year I'll Be Special

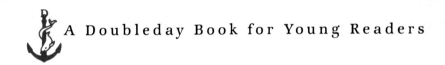 A Doubleday Book for Young Readers

Next Year

...'ll Be Special

by PATRICIA REILLY GIFF

pictures by MARYLIN HAFNER

A Doubleday Book for Young Readers
Published by
Delacorte Press
Bantam Doubleday Dell Publishing Group, Inc.
1540 Broadway
New York, New York 10036
Doubleday and the portrayal of an anchor with a dolphin are trademarks
of Bantam Doubleday Dell Publishing Group, Inc.

Library of Congress Cataloging in Publication Data

Giff, Patricia Reilly.
 Next year I'll be special / by Patricia Reilly Giff ; pictures by Marylin
Hafner.
  p.   cm.
 Summary: Unhappy at school, Marilyn fantasizes about how much
better life will be next year when she is in the second grade.
  ISBN 0-385-30903-1
 [1. Schools—Fiction.]   I. Hafner, Marylin, ill.   II. Title.
 PZ7.G3626Ne   1993 [E]—dc20   92-20749   CIP   AC

Manufactured in the United States of America
September 1993
10 9 8 7 6 5 4 3 2 1

WOR

for Alice because she's special
and for teachers who make
children feel special
          P.R.G.

for Abby, Jennifer, & Amanda
                M.H.

Next year, when I'm in second grade,
I won't have mean Miss Minch anymore.
Everything will be different.

Miss Lark will be my teacher.
She has long curly hair and crinkly eyes,
and Wendy says she never yells.

As soon as
Miss Lark sees me,
she'll know I'm special.
    "Marilyn," she'll say,
"would you like to be
the board washer,
or the door monitor,
or my desk duster,
or the messenger?"

"Yes," I'll say,
"I'll be all of them."

When it's time for reading,
Miss Lark will say,
"Marilyn, why are you reading
with the bottom group?

"Anyone can see
you're the best reader in the class
when someone helps you
with the hard words."

In math, no one will notice
when I count on my fingers,
except Miss Lark,
and she'll just wink at me.
I won't have to rush.
I'll get all the answers right.

And Gina will say to Richard,
"Did you notice
how smart Marilyn is this year?"

When we line up for recess,
Christine will say, "I want
to stand next to Marilyn."
Linda will frown.
"No," she'll say. "It's my turn."
"Don't fight over me, girls,"
I'll say.

"Christine can stand in front of me
and Linda can stand in back of me."
But Karen will say, "What about me?
I want to stand next to Marilyn too."

Outside, Helen will say,
"Marilyn, why are you taking
the end of the jump rope?
We want you to be first jumper."
Connie will say,
"Marilyn never misses.
She's the best jumper in the class."

All the girls and half the boys
will want to share their snacks with me.
Mary Kate will hand me her candy bar.
    "Oh, Marilyn," she'll say.
"Not such a little bite.
Take a big one."

And Eric will give me his orange,
the juicy kind I love.

Even Mark will want to share
his hard-boiled egg.

"No, thank you very much," I'll say.
(I HATE eggs.)

In art I will draw a beautiful picture,
all yellow and green.

Mrs. Caro, the art teacher, will say,
"That picture is lovely.
I'm going to hang it in the hall.
All the visitors will see it."

Susan will tell Billy,
"Marilyn has fourteen pictures
hanging in the hall now."

The music teacher will ask me
to come to the piano.

"Will you sing for us, Marilyn?"
he'll ask.

Then I'll sing a song
in my A-plus voice.

"Are you going to be an opera singer
when you grow up?" the teacher will ask.

"No," I'll say,
"I'm going to be a movie star."

There are twenty-four children
in my class, not counting me.

On Valentine's Day,
I'll get twenty-four cards
in the Valentine Box.
Everyone will want to be my valentine.

When we pack our books to go home
in the afternoon, I'll tell Miss Lark,
"You forgot to give us homework.
Miss Minch always gave us a hundred pages."

"Oh dear," Miss Lark will say.
"Read some of your library book.
I hope you enjoy it."

I'll be invited
to so many birthday parties
that my mother will say,
"Marilyn, I've bought
twenty-four birthday presents
this year. You must be
the most popular girl in the class."
    "What can I do?" I'll smile.
"Everyone wants me."

Daddy will say,
"Marilyn, you look different this year."

"I am different, Daddy," I'll say.
"This year I'm special."

"Oh, Marilyn," he'll say with a smile.
"You were always special to me."

Next year,
mean Miss Minch will still be in first grade.

I'll be in second with Miss Lark.
And everything will be different.

PATRICIA REILLY GIFF

is the author of numerous picture books and works of fiction for children, including the popular Kids of the Polk Street School books and the Lincoln Lions Band books. As a former reading consultant and elementary-school teacher, she has known many children and teachers who wished things were different. She wrote this book hoping that "everyone who reads it will try to make other people feel special." She lives in Weston, Connecticut.

MARYLIN HAFNER

has illustrated many books for children, including *Red Day, Green Day* by Edith Kurhardt and *Raymond's Best Summer* by Jean Rogers. She lives in Cambridge, Massachusetts.

The text of this book is set in 16-point Zapf International Medium.
Typography by Lynn Braswell.